SECRET
OF THE PAST

by Miriam Schlein

Illustrated by Kees de Kiefte

A
LITTLE APPLE
PAPERBACK

SCHOLASTIC INC.
New York Toronto London Auckland Sydney

ISBN 0-590-45701-2

Copyright © 1992 by Miriam Schlein.
Illustrations copyright © 1992 by Scholastic Inc.
All rights reserved. Published by Scholastic Inc.
APPLE PAPERBACKS is a registered trademark of Scholastic Inc.

12 11 10 9 8 7 6 5 4 3 2   2 3 4 5 6 7/9

Printed in the U.S.A.   40

First Scholastic printing, September 1992

1.

A Change in Plan

I really wanted to go to baseball camp with Fats Henderson. Fats is my best friend. He doesn't mind — we all call him Fats. He says Fats is better than Willie. His real name is William.

Anyway, we heard about this great camp, and we're all set to go. We got the okay from our folks, and it doesn't cost a lot.

This camp's supposed to make you a great player. So, we're bunting, and throwing knuckleballs, and practicing stuff till it gets dark every night. We want to be pretty good when we get there. We don't want to look like dopes. In fact, we're so busy with all this that Fats doesn't even look fat after a while.

Soon we're really in great shape. Then, what happens? My folks put the kibosh on the whole deal.

One night I come in all sweaty. My cleats are muddy. My bat falls with a crash. Usually all these things give my mother the willies. But this time she doesn't even notice — the bat, the sweat, the cleats. Nothing.

"Darling," she says. "The most wonderful thing has happened. I'm so excited. I know you will be, too."

She hugs me. She still is paying no attention to the mud, the sweat, the cleats. Boy, this must be something.

"Your father is attending a conference in Bolivia. It's very last minute. And his family is invited. We're going to Bolivia!"

"Mom! I'm going to baseball camp with Fats."

"Oh, Albert honey, you can do that next year. This is something special. Who do you know who's been to Bolivia?"

Well, she's got me there. Nobody.

I guess you know how this ends. On

Thursday, Fats gets on the bus to the Poconos looking half happy, half glum. And on Saturday, my mom and dad drag me down to Bolivia, South America, of all places. *All* glum.

On the plane, I'm trying to take some pictures of the clouds, and my mom is talking about this and that. "We're invited to stay with the Valdezes," she says. "Remember? I told you. They have a son your age, who you can play with."

I don't mean to sound like a pill. My mom is really nice. But sometimes she lapses into sandbox talk. "Play with!" What does she think I am, in kindergarten?

"I really feel I let Fats down," I grumble.

I think at this point my folks are getting pretty fed up with me. My father leans across the aisle. "I think Fats will survive," he says. Then he goes back to his papers.

My dad's an energy expert. He gets asked to advise companies, and even countries. But usually we — me and Mom — don't get to go with him. It just happened this time.

I thought it would be interesting in a plane. I never flew before. But it turns out it's something like riding in a bus, only there's nothing to see outside. A lady comes up and down the aisle and keeps giving me stuff. 7-Up. Peanuts. Then some food on a square plate that didn't taste like much. I was sorry I didn't get more peanuts.

When we touched down, the Valdezes were there in full force to greet us. I don't know why I was so tired. It was only about three o'clock.

"It's the altitude," said Mr. Valdez.

"The air is thin," said Mrs. Valdez.

"You get used to it," said the kid with them. This must be the one I was supposed to "play with."

"Lay-oh," he says then and sticks out his hand.

"Lay-oh?" I figure maybe it's some kind of Bolivian greeting.

He grins. "It's my name. L-E-O."

I get it. L<u>ee</u>-oh.

"Al," I say, We shake.

"Leonardo," says his mother proudly.

Oh, boy.

Leo was small; very thin, not skinny, wiry, really. His hair was so black, it was almost blue. I couldn't believe he was my age, though. He was so small.

The streets of La Paz were jam-packed with people. They were cooking food and selling all kinds of stuff. To tell the truth, it looked kind of interesting. I thought I could dump my bag at the house. Then Leo and I could look around.

It didn't work out that way. Turns out we couldn't go anyplace. Instead, we sat around all day, sipping tea. Tea, for Pete's sake!

"You can't do anything the first day," my dad said. "Because of the thin air. We're really high in the mountains."

"Mountain air has less oxygen in it," said Mr. Valdez. "The tea helps you get used to it."

Leo's mom chimed in. "People get sick if they try and do too much at first."

"It's true," said Leo. "They vomit. They get headaches. They get nosebleeds. They . . ."

"Enough!" said his mom. "Alberto, have some more tea."

Ugh!

But I was polite and took it.

The next day I felt fine, ready to explore. But as it turns out, we were leaving La Paz. That afternoon we all took off in a small propeller plane.

This ride was more fun. We flew so low, we could look down and really see things. Some llamas on a mountain trail. Two kids feeding a pig. In half an hour, we coasted in for a landing near a small mountain village. Not the kind of place my dad usually goes to for conferences. But I wasn't even asking questions anymore.

Leo and I got along fine. He spoke really good English. But when he got excited and got to talking fast, he spoke a mix of Spanish, English, and Quechua (KECH-wuh) —

which is a Bolivian Indian language. I couldn't even understand straight Spanish, let alone a Spanish and Indian mix.

It turns out that Leo was miffed, too. Seems that he was all set to go on a llama hiking trip in the mountains with his buddies from school. And then his mom and dad pull this deal on him, the same as mine. Why are they like that, parents?

The first day, Leo and I got to go out on our own. The thing is, there wasn't much to do here. The place was real small. There were some girls weaving stuff right in the street. There was a little one-room museum with some bones all laid out in cases. Looking at the weaving and bones took a good fifteen minutes. Leo and I looked at each other. What now?

Then, coming out from behind the museum, we saw a guy walking along with a loaded llama. That's when I got my great idea.

"Hey," I said, "why don't we go on a hike — without a llama. We can carry our own stuff. Look at the mountains. This is a great place to hike!"

Leo was doubtful. "It's pretty wild country," he said. "There are jaguars. Snakes, too."

"We won't go far. It'll be like a picnic. We'll get some cheese and bread and take our water canteens. Come on."

I grabbed him by the arm. It didn't take much convincing, really. He was as bored as I was.

We went back to the house. We didn't have knapsacks, so we stuffed the cheese and bread in our pockets. I stuck a pencil in my pocket, too, because I like to draw, and you never know when the urge will strike. We set out up the main street. We forgot one very important thing, though. Our canteen of water. Looking back, that's what was the beginning of all our trouble, if you want to call it that.

2.

The Hike

The main street dribbled down into nothing pretty soon. Not exactly nothing. It became a trail. Sometimes we could hardly see it. We began hearing some pretty weird noises. Screams and shrieks. This didn't bother us. Leo told me what they were. They were parrots and macaws. Sometimes we heard a whirr, and saw them flash by — yellow and red and blue — really bright colors. If you used those colors in art class, everyone would say yyecch . . . gross. But, here, on the birds, they were really stupendous.

Sometimes we heard sort of faint snuffling noises. In the village there were some animals. Pigs and sheep, which just wandered around. But these didn't sound like pigs or sheep. We couldn't see anything because thick vines twisted down to the ground.

"Let's go back," said Leo. Even though he is from Bolivia, Leo is more of a city kid than I am.

To tell the truth, I was beginning to agree with Leo. There's such a thing as being too macho. Mr. Valdez is an important man here. He's the Minister of Energy. How would it look if I got his son lost, and they had to come search for us? I didn't want to muck up my dad's credibility. That's a word they sling around a lot in my house. If you don't have it, it means people can't count on you. I didn't want to really mess things up for him.

"I guess you're right," I said.

Leo sure looked relieved. He seemed to perk up instantly. "But let's eat first," he said. "Look. there's a clear spot. Near those rocks."

"Good idea."

To get to the clearing we had to go off

the trail a bit. We pulled out our cheese and bread, which had gotten kind of mushed up in our pockets. It tasted pretty good anyhow.

It was a kind of overlook we were on. Leaning against the rocks, we looked out over a valley. Sitting there, munching on the bread and cheese, I felt somehow like an explorer. Little did I know.

"Hey, I'm thirsty." Leo's English was really good. Better than mine. He spoke like someone from England. He learned to talk that way at some special school he went to. I was the one who taught him things like "Hey." I didn't know how his folks would feel about it.

I looked around. "Where's the canteen?"

He thought I had it.

I thought he had it.

We discovered we just didn't have it. Period.

Leo stood up. "There's a stream down there. You see it? I'm going down for a drink."

"You think it's okay?"

He looked at me, surprised. "Why not?"

I guess they don't have pollution and toxic stuff up here in the mountains.

I shrugged. "Okay."

Leo led the way. I followed.

He lay down on his belly to drink, sucking up the water in slurps. Something told me I should wait. So I kept waiting. I guess it was instinct — or common sense — that told me both of us lying down at once would make us too vulnerable.

And, boy, was I right.

As he slurped, I looked around. And I saw it. It looked like a small tiger. Only it was solid black. It was poised on the rocks like a statue. Not moving.

"Leo," I whispered, poking him gently with my foot. "Look up. To the left."

He lifted his head slowly.

"Jaguar." He breathed out the word. "I'm going to get up slowly, very slowly. There's a cleft in the rocks, back there. Did you see

it? We can squeeze in there. If we can barricade it . . ."

I'm thinking, Suppose the jag waits us out. With another part of my brain, I'm thinking, This Leo is some cool dude.

"Remember. Don't bolt." Leo hesitates. "Unless we have to."

Leo gets up. I start backing up. All in slow motion.

Everything's fine. We're halfway to the hidey-hole. Then, wouldn't you know it. Before I can even try to hold it in, I give out a big sneeze.

That did it. The jag leaps. We make a dash. We pelt into that crevice like two bullets. At the edge of it, Leo stumbles. I grab him around the waist and pull.

We're both in.

Surprise, surprise. It's not a crack in the rocks. It's more like a cave. A kind of hidden hole in the ground. We start falling. The last thing I see is the jag, pawing and snorting outside. He could have fit in and gotten us, easy. But he doesn't seem to want to. He must know something that's keeping him out of here.

Held together, sort of, since I'm still hanging onto Leo, we slip down, down, down — out of this world, it seems.

3.

Down the Cave-Hole

It was not really a hole. It was more like a down-sloping cave — steep, but not totally vertical. If it had been, we would have been goners because it was deep. We must have slid down five or six hundred feet, at least. We rolled, tumbled, and bounced for I don't know how long. We both must have passed out on the way. I don't even remember hitting bottom.

I was the first to open my eyes. There was light down here. The cave-hole had an opening at this end. I blinked a few times and looked out.

My first thought was, wow! This must be some kind of open zoo. There were animals all over the place. My second thought was, I must be dreaming. Because they were the

17

weirdest animals I had ever seen.

Over by some trees was a huge hairy orange thing. It was standing on its back legs, zapping up leaves with its tongue. Big? You better believe it. It was taller than the trees. It had a lump on its back. The lump began to move. It was a baby orange thing. The baby was as big as a bear.

Right near us, a bunch of camel-like animals were wandering around. They looked almost ordinary. Except they had no humps. But they had super-long necks. Come to think of it, they looked more like giraffes than camels. Except they were a solid tan.

Off to the side was something else again. It looked like a cross between a gigantic armadillo and a dragon. A strange combo, you gotta admit. It was round-bodied. Big. Scaly. And about as big as an elephant. Sticking out from underneath were feet that made hippo feet look like twigs. And it had a thick tail. At the end of the tail was a ball with spikes on it.

I suppose you don't believe me. Well, I don't blame you. 'Cause I didn't believe myself. So I did what you're supposed to do to test out whether you're dreaming. I pinched myself. I felt the pinch. What does that mean? Does it mean I'm not dreaming?

Just then, Leo gave a moan. "Ooooohhh . . ." He had a lump on the side of his head the size of an egg. When Leo moaned, the gigantic armadillo-thing turned in our direction.

If it heard Leo's moan, does that mean all this is real . . . and I'm not dreaming? To tell the truth, I wasn't in such wonderful shape myself to do any heavy thinking.

Then I figured it out. These must be regular South American animals that I just never happened to see in a zoo. Hey, if you saw an elephant or a giraffe for the first time, you would think it's pretty weird looking, wouldn't you?

Leo could settle this whole question. But he's still out like a light.

And, speaking of elephants, here they come. A bunch of them. They had been hidden behind some trees. Maybe this is a circus grounds. You know, where they stay over in winter. Like they do in Florida.

I love elephants. They're so calm and strong. Careful not to disturb Leo, I half stood up to get a better look. Oh, man! I couldn't stand. My left ankle was blown up like a balloon.

These sure were weird-looking elephants. Their tusks were sort of curlicued — almost like a corkscrew. Suddenly, another bunch of elephants came out from behind some rocks. This is really the limit. These have four tusks!

Maybe I'm not dreaming. Maybe I have a concussion, and I'm seeing double. Or hallucinating.

Just as I'm doing my elephant-watching, Leo opens his eyes. First thing he says is, "Water . . ." Second thing he says, as he gets a chance to look around, is "Dios mio!" And he grabs me so tight, I think the circulation is cut off from my arm.

Well, there goes my dream theory. Because Leo sees the same stuff I do. Can two people have the same dream at the same time? I doubt it. And there goes my circus theory, too. These are not run-of-the-mill ordinary South American animals. Because Leo's eyes are popping out of his skull with shock.

4.

Hidden Land
of the Past

"Where are we?"

A good question.

Leo put his hand gingerly up to his goose egg. After his first look, Leo is not paying any more attention to the huge hairy orange thing, the dragon-armadillo, and the weird-looking elephants. Because he is *sure* he's hallucinating.

"I don't feel well," he says. "I want to go home."

Yeah. Tell me about it.

Then he faints again. He's a deadweight on my shoulder. His face is awfully white. And the lump on his head is turning blue.

In a couple of seconds, his eyes pop open.

"Let's get out of here," he says suddenly in a loud voice. He pulls away from me. I don't know where his strength is coming from. Where does he want to go? Out there? With the animals? It's all I can do to hold him down.

Meanwhile, something's going on out there. Before, it was a sort of peaceful scene. Now, the hairy orange thing has gotten down from her hind legs. She is peering around. The elephants are grouped together and waving their trunks in the air. The giraffe-camel animals have suddenly dashed off. Only the armadillo-dragon thing is standing there calm as a clam.

The elephants begin moving closer. Is it us that's getting them nervous? Do they smell us? Did they hear Leo yell? Can they reach in here? In spite of thinking that this may be the last two minutes of my life, I can't help but stare. I've never seen elephants like that before — with four tusks. It's got to be some different, unknown type. I take out my pencil to make a little drawing.

I don't have any paper. So I draw it on my shirtsleeve.

Then, out of the corner of my eye, I see what's getting them all nervous. It's up on a rock. It has huge fangs curving out of its mouth. I know what this is. I've seen it. Only pictures of it in books, mind you. Never for real. It's a saber-toothed cat.

I kid you not.

I also know this. Saber-tooth has been extinct for a million years.

Now saber-tooth leaps down and bounces along toward the elephants. The armadillo-dragon thing is standing in its path. Right before my eyes it lashes out with its spike-tail. It whacks saber-tooth in the chest.

Saber-tooth is knocked cold. Is it dead? I'm sure not going out there to find out.

As all this is going on, the elephants have started to run straight toward us. I don't think they are after us. I think they are going to make a stand against saber-tooth with their backs to the rock wall. Now, with saber-tooth knocked out, they don't have to. But one of them hasn't stopped running soon enough. He hits the wall. A small bit of his tusk breaks off.

Now, suddenly, everything is calm again. All the other animals have wandered off to some other spot, leaving the conked-out saber-tooth in solitary splendor.

I stared at saber-tooth. Suddenly I knew we had made a discovery unparalleled by any-thing — even the guys going up to the moon. What we fell into was a piece of the past pre-served. By some freak of chance, here, down in this "hole," a part of the world remained just the way it was a million years ago.

Leo and I have fallen into a hidden land of the past.

5.

A Long Haul

How big was this place? And how was it able to stay this way? Right now, these were academic questions. Because bravery is not my strong point. And I wasn't going out there for anything. I knew if we wanted to stay alive, we had only one choice. We had to creep up through that sloping cave-hole that we fell down through. Back to our own world.

But before trying to get back, there was one thing I couldn't resist. I reached out and grabbed that twisty bit of broken-off elephant tusk and stuck it in my pocket.

We. Did I say *we* had to creep up? I meant *I* had to creep up. Leo was still unconscious. I had to get both of us up. Could I do it?

There was only one way to find out. I took hold of Leo's arm and began creeping.

It was slow going.

They say, "Whatever goes up, must come down." But no one ever says, "Whatever goes down, must come up."

The sloping tunnel had no headroom. Because of my ankle, I couldn't stand up anyhow. Crawling was all I could do. So, on my knees and on one hand (the other hand gripping Leo), I began the slow climb. How far did we have to go this way? I didn't even want to think about it.

One thing was good, though. The air in the tunnel was fresh. There must have been openings to the outside at some other places in the tunnel, other than at the top and bottom.

Soon my hands and knees began to get very sore. I decided to rip up my shirt and put wrappings around my knees and around the hand that I was "walking" on.

I didn't know how long this tunnel was. We had no food. And worse — no water. I read someplace that you can go without food for a long time. But not without water. And at the rate I was going, who knew how long it would take me to get us out? But I didn't let myself think thoughts like that.

Poor Leo. How was he doing? Not great. As I dragged him, he was getting an awful bumping around. He would mumble something every once in a while, so I knew he wasn't in a coma or anything. But being dragged along like this was not the greatest thing in the world for someone with a head injury. I stopped to catch my breath, and to think. What I decided was to try to carry Leo on my back. Good thing he was such a little wiry guy. Gently, I put him on my back. I couldn't hold him. So I tied him onto me with his belt. Now I could creep using both hands. This way, I moved along a lot faster.

One of the scary things was, it was really dark black in here. I'm not really scared of the dark. That's not what bothered me. But suppose the hole we had fallen down branched off in different directions? Suppose I was creeping up some other pathway, to a dead end? It was no good letting myself think things like that.

Finally I got so tired, I untied Leo and stretched out, with Leo's head resting on my arm. I put my face down close to his mouth to try to find out if he was still breathing. He was.

Oh, God . . . you read about all sorts of adventures like this when you're sitting home, safe, with your mom in the next room, and your dog lying at your feet . . . and a refrigerator in the kitchen filled with food.

I'm not ashamed to admit this. I cried myself to sleep.

6.

Amigos

It's always hard to figure things out the minute you wake up. I opened my eyes. At first, I thought I was on a camping trip. Why did I think that?

A stream. I heard something that sounded like a stream.

I had a piece of string in my pocket. I tied one end of it to Leo's wrist, and held onto the other end. (I didn't want to lose him in the dark.) Then I headed toward the sound.

The tunnel seemed wider here. It was also higher. The stream was just about ten feet away. It gushed out of a waist-high hole, ran along for a short distance, then disappeared into a slit in the rock.

Not knowing what to expect, I stuck just

the tip of my finger in it first. For all I knew, it could be molten lava! But no. Glory be, it was just plain water. What am I talking about, "just plain water"? It was glorious, wonderful ice-cold water! I bent down to drink, then dunked my head in, then my arms and legs, to try to unstiffen them.

Cupping my hands, I carried some water over to Leo.

"Leo," I said.

Nothing.

If someone's unconscious, I don't think you're supposed to give him anything to drink. But I washed off his face and head.

Suddenly something touched my leg. I looked down. It was Leo's hand. Then I heard him mumble something. "Amigo," he said.

"Amigo," I answered. "Don't worry. We'll make it."

I went back for some more water. He took a few sips and fell asleep.

I let him rest awhile. Then I figured we had to get moving. I drank some more. I tried to figure out how I could carry some water with us. No way. I had nothing to carry it in. Then I got an idea.

I took off my pants, wet them in the stream, and put them back on again. It felt terrible. But if we got desperate, I could ring them out and get some water. Not exactly Miss Manners. But, then, again, this was no garden party. And if it could save our lives, what the heck.

I strapped Leo onto my back with the belt and once again headed up the tunnel.

7.

Return of
Humongous-Orange

When I say "up the tunnel," I really mean up. I was not just creeping with someone on my back. That would be hard enough. As I was creeping, I was climbing uphill. Some places, it must have been a 40-degree upward slant. Luckily, it was not always that steep. A good thing I went through all that training with Fats. It toughened me up.

I wondered how Fats was doing at baseball camp. Grousing about this and that, I'd bet. Food no good. Coach too strict. I could just imagine. Fats was a grouser. If I get out of here, I thought, I'll never grouse again.

To pass the time, I decided to count steps.

Or creeps. I got to 350 and decided to call it quits. One blessing. The ground was not rocky. It was soft and fluffy. Not like sand. More like dust.

Three or four times, where it was less steep, I stopped to rest. I kept Leo tied to me at all times. By his wrist. I didn't want him rolling back down.

Each time, before starting off, I resumed my counting. Just to keep my mind off everything else. At 950 I got to a really level stretch. I checked on Leo. He didn't look any better or worse than before. I fell asleep again.

As the guy in Shakespeare says, "To sleep, perchance to dream . . . Aye, and there's the rub." Which means, as Ms. Wickenden explained in Special Lit. 02, even when we sleep, we can't escape things, 'cause our problems follow us into our dreams.

And, boy, is that true. What I dreamed about was the humongous hairy orange thing. It was coming toward me. Closer.

Closer. I tried to run away, but I couldn't.
Then it stuck its big tongue out.

I screamed.

You know how things in dreams some-times make you wake up? I woke myself up with my scream. I opened my eyes.

And a tongue was really licking my face. I screamed again, and passed out.

8.

Is This Heaven?

When I opened my eyes, I saw clouds and blue sky. Was I in heaven? Then I heard a dog bark, and I figured no. I had the idea there were no dogs in heaven. Though come to think of it, it would probably be nicer with dogs up there.

Two guys were staring down at us, looking as surprised to see us as I was to see them. They were for real. Behind them I saw trees . . . and a llama . . . and a dog. It must have been their dog that licked me. I wanted to jump up and hug them all. Instead I burst out crying.

We made it.

We were out!

They started talking in some strange language. Probably Quechua. It sounded

nice — almost like they were singing. I took a look at Leo. I could see why the men looked so startled. Leo was totally black. The soft dusty stuff in the tunnel must have been black.

I looked at my arm. I was the same way.

The last time I fell asleep, we must have been out of the tunnel. But because it happened to be night, I just didn't know it.

The guys made a stretcher out of branches, and carried Leo down the mountain. I got to ride on the llama.

9.

"There Are No Elephants in Bolivia!"

You never know how people are going to react to things. My dad, old toughie that he was, began sobbing when he saw me. My mom just said "Oh!" and grabbed me in a crusher. I guess they never expected to see me again.

They fixed me up. Bandages around my hands, elbows, and knees — *you* try mountain-climbing on your hands and knees. Stickum around my left ankle. I had sprained it in the fall down. I knew it hurt. But I hadn't paid much attention to it. There's only a certain amount of attention your brain can muster up. And with everything else going on, my ankle was the least of it.

Me? You'd think I would be the happiest person in the world. The crazy thing is — I didn't want to talk to anybody. Me. The big talker.

I didn't ask how long we had been gone. I didn't say a word about any of the stuff we saw. It was weird.

I heard all these low conversations that always stopped when I came near. ". . . The boy's in shock . . ." they would say. . . . ". . . normal reaction . . . trauma. . . ." And so on.

Mostly it was Leo they were worried about. He lay there with his head bandaged up like a mummy. He had a fever of 106, and slipped in and out of consciousness. When he was conscious, boy, you knew it. Quiet, shy Leo either shouted or talked a mile a minute.

Some special doctor, a big fat guy, flew in from La Paz by helicopter. Now no one could get to go in and see Leo but the doc, the nurse, and his mom and dad. I wasn't allowed in. But from out in the hall I could hear him yelling, "Tigre! Perdido!" Sometimes he went into long speeches. I could make out some words. He was talking about everything. The hole. The fall. The elephants. He talked a mile a minute about "the big lump with the killer tail."

Of course they thought he was delirious and making everything up. He went in and out of different languages. Sometimes he hollered for me. "Alberto! Ayuda! Watch out!"

They never once let me in there. They said I'd get him overexcited. Man! How could I get him more overexcited than he was?

His mom avoided me altogether. I knew she had the idea everything was all my fault. Heck. I saved Leo's life. But she didn't know that.

"But how did he get hurt?" they asked me over and over.

I tried to explain everything to them. About the jaguar. And the cave-hole. How deep it was. And about the hidden land. But every time I got to the part about the animals — especially the elephants — they all just looked at each other and sort of stopped listening. As if to say, "Oh yeah. Elephants. Because as you know, and I know, and everybody knows, there *are* no elephants in Bolivia." Well, that's what *they* think.

One day somebody else turned up. A young guy. It seems he worked in a museum someplace. And he got to go in to see Leo. He was in there a good long time. Why was *he* allowed in? I couldn't even go in for a minute.

I just sat there at the edge of the veranda. I don't think they even saw me when they all trooped out and settled down for a confab.

Museum guy: "Leo's descriptions are amazingly accurate — for a boy as sick as he is. . . ." He looks down at his notes and ticks them off:

"The jumbo armadillo, what he calls 'the big lump with the killer tail.' This is *Glyptodon*. Five meters long. Weight: two tons. Ball of spikes on tail.

"His 'tigre.' This is *Smilodon*. Better-known as saber-tooth cat. Huge canines curving down from upper jaw.

"The gigantic orange monster he talked about — that's the giant ground sloth *Megatherium*. Six meters long. Thick, reddish-brown hair. Browsed from treetops.

"And the spiral-tusked elephants he describes . . . that's the mastodon *Cordillerion,* which used to roam the Andes."

He scratched his nose thoughtfully. "Of course you know the boys could not have seen these animals. They've all been extinct for thousands of years."

They all look at each other, trying to make sense out of all this.

Then the doc pipes up. "It's a form of hallucination, bringing in learned rather than experiential data. . . ."

Mr. Valdez, proudly: "Of course the boy's a big reader. . . ."

His mom: "And he remembers everything."

Right then something snaps. I pop out of my self-imposed silence. "Of course he remembers," I say. "He saw them only a few days ago!"

They all turn to look at me, so surprised, it was as though the table had suddenly spoken.

"And I've got *proof* we saw those elephants," I add, suddenly remembering the tusk bit I had picked up. "Here . . . here in my pocket."

I feel around, then realize of course I wasn't wearing the same pants. I leap up. "Where are my pants? You know. The ones I was wearing?"

My mom is delighted to hear me talking at long last. "Sweetheart. You mean those wet filthy things? We had to cut them off you. Literally cut them off you."

49

"Where are they?" I yelled.

"We threw them out," said my mom. "Why would we save them?"

I spent the next three days rooting around in the town garbage, looking for my pants. I gave up when, knee-deep in rinds, bones, and eggshells, it became a contest between me and an unfriendly-looking, rather large, yellow-spotted snake.

I decided I'd have to take a different tack.

10.

Another Piece
of the Puzzle

The next week I spent most of my time at the little museum. Along with the bones and clay pots, it had a room with a lot of old books. These were only supposed to be used by adults. But I got special permission, through Mr. Valdez.

The books were so old, sometimes the edges of the pages would crumble in your hand. It was slow going. I plowed through an awful lot of books. I couldn't read them. They were in Spanish. But I knew what I was looking for. Pictures. Finally I found them. In a book called *Los Ultimos Días del Pleistocene*. My Spanish dictionary told me

this means "The Final Days of the Pleistocene." My English dictionary told me that
the Pleistocene Age was the time from two
million to about 10,000 years ago.

I couldn't read any of it. But the pictures!
The pictures told me everything. That Leo
and I were not loco. Of course I never
thought that for a minute. But, still, when

GLYPTODON

SMILODON

AEPYCAMELUS

52

nobody believes you, you get to wonder after a while.

Bingo! There they were. All of them.

The humongous orange thing. The armadillo-dragon spike-tailed thing. The elephants with twisty tusks. The giraffe-camel thing. And saber-tooth.

I copied the pictures into my notebook.

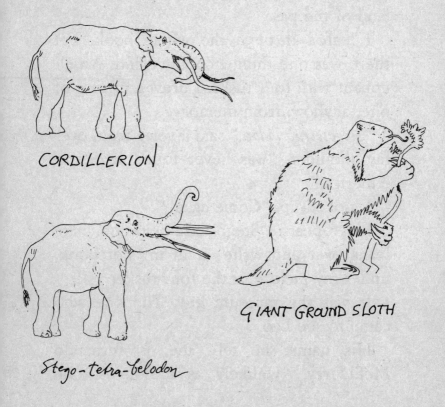

CORDILLERION

GIANT GROUND SLOTH

Stego-tetra-belodon

I put the proper scientific name under each one.

Of course we still had a problem. A big problem. How were we going to prove that they weren't extinct? That they were all still alive and well. Living down there, safe and sound, at the bottom of the cave-hole. Hidden from everybody . . . down in that secret land of the past.

I leafed through the whole book, but there was one thing I couldn't find. An elephant with four tusks. I drew a picture of one, anyhow, from memory.

"*Stegotetrabelodon*," said a voice from over my shoulder, "was never found in South America."

I looked up. "Come again?"

He repeats. "Stego-tetra-belo-don." He leans over and writes it in my notebook, under my picture of the four-tusker.

It was the museum guy. The one who came to see Leo.

His name, he tells me, is Fernando McElderry. "Unlikely as it sounds," he adds, and sticks out a hand for me to shake.

I shake it. I like it when grown-ups treat you like a real person.

He points to my picture of the four-tusked stego-whatever. "These never lived in South America. Only in Africa."

Oh, yeah? I think. But I let that go for the moment. I latch onto another idea. "But all the others did. Right? Saber-tooth? The Glypto-thing? Hairy orange? The twirly-tusks? And that camel-whatever?"

He didn't answer. But I saw that he was doing some heavy thinking.

So I went on. "Is this what you're saying?" — I paused dramatically. (It was not for nothing that I spent a year in the drama club!) — "That maybe it's possible we really *did* see all the other things. But not the four-tuskers?"

Then I struck home. "Maybe," I said, "the four-tuskers *were* here. But nobody knows that. None of the scientists. The experts. Nobody. But me and Leo, we know it."

We sat there for a minute.

"And you," I added. "Now you know it. If you believe me."

Still without answering, Fernando took me to the other museum room and pointed to something in a glass case.

My eyes popped. It was the tusk piece — all curlicued and twirly; the one that I grabbed, down in the land of the past.

"That's mine!" I said. "It's what got thrown out with my pants!"

I looked at the card in the case:

TUSK FRAGMENT. CORDILLERION. AGE: 2 million years.

Fernando shook his head. "No," he said, "we've had this a long time. My dad found it in 1957. It was a rare find. A lot of the big museums wanted it. But he felt it should stay right here."

Now I was really interested. Here was another piece of the puzzle. But how, exactly, did it fit in?

"Where did he find it?"

"Down in the Mescalana Valley. Below Yago Point. Not far from here."

"He found it right out in the open?"

"I guess so. He never did pinpoint the location for me exactly."

Then Fernando unlocked the case, took the piece out, and handed it to me. I realized he was doing something special for me. Now, holding it, I knew it was bigger than the piece I had picked up. I rubbed my thumb along the twisty edge.

And I began to wonder: Had Fernando's dad somehow found his way down to the hidden land of the past, too? Was his tusk piece really as old as it said on the card? Or was it from the present, like the one I had? How could you tell?

So I asked. Fernando was the kind of guy you could ask things, and not feel like a dope.

"How do you know it's two million years old? Instead of, say, thirty years old?"

Fernando explained about something called the argon potassium dating system. I can't remember the details. But I guess they really can tell how old something is.

A thought struck me. If I still had my tusk piece, they could have tested it. That could *prove* it was brand new. Then they would have to believe us. But I guess what's gone is gone.

Drat!

11.

Accidental Explorers

Good news! Leo hit a turning point. The crisis, they called it. Believe me, everybody was tiptoeing around for a while. We didn't know if he was going to make it. But he did. And after that, he got better pretty fast. His mom was so happy, she even started talking to me again.

One day, Mr. Valdez said he had a surprise. What was the surprise? Us! Me and Leo. We were supposed to give a lecture. About our "adventure," as he called it. Not to a big crowd. Just at home.

Mr. Valdez set it up all formal. We sat behind a long table, facing our audience. You'd think we were giving a lecture at Harvard or something. The only thing was, we

sat instead of stood. 'Cause Leo was still pretty weak.

And of course it was just a mini-audience: My mom and dad. Mr. and Mrs. Valdez. And Fernando McElderry. Who, it turns out, is Leo's godfather. Being so young, he's sort of like Leo's big brother. He is also a mammalogist — which is a fancy word for animal expert.

So there we were. Leo and me, spouting off. The two accidental explorers. We told them, again — for around the hundredth time — every single thing that happened. Stopping by the stream. Getting a drink. The black jaguar. The cave-hole. The big fall. And, of course, the animals. We described every detail we could remember.

They all listened.

Not that they believed us.

But it seems the medico said it was better for us to "get it all out." "To ventilate our fantasies."

Whatever that means.

Bunk!

That's why we were there — talking about stuff no one believed.

Except maybe Fernando McElderry. He was really listening. He even recorded us on tape. I had the feeling he almost sort of believed us.

Leo talked mostly about how we happened to get down there. And I told about how we got up. 'Cause, as you know, all the way back Leo was out like a light.

I told about the stream in the cave. And how I soaked my pants for emergency water. (My dad nodded proudly at that part.) I explained how I strapped Leo onto my back. (At this point, his mom started sniffling and wiping her eyes.)

I told about the guys who found us. And how we were completely covered with black dust.

All this time Fernando's been scribbling notes. Now he looks up.

"Black dust?"

I must say, Fernando gets interested in the oddest things.

Then I got to the very end. About my horrible dream, but how it was really the dog licking me. About how the guys made a stretcher for Leo. And how I rode home on the llama.

We got up. Our parents hugged us.

Leo's mom grabs me in a bear hug. "You will be like another son to me!" she says.

Of course I did save Leo. But I didn't know I was going to get such a reward — or punishment — as an extra mom!

12.

Fernando's Theory

"What's so great about black dust?" I ask Fernando when I get a chance.

"It's volcanic dust."

"So?"

Suddenly he goes into some long-winded story. "A couple of years ago, I read a sort of unusual book. It was science fiction. It took place in prehistoric times. It tells about a tremendous volcanic eruption. The ground shifts. A large wedge of earth sinks and gets covered up. Everything living there drops out of sight. Including the animals. But they have all they need to live. Air. Food. Water. Vegetation. So they live on, for tens of thousands of years — right into modern times.

And no one knows they're there. It's a preserved Ice Age biome."

Leo and I look at each other.

"What's the name of this book?" I say. "I'd like to read it."

Leo chimes in. "Yes. Get it for me, Nando." He looks at me. "It's probably in Spanish. I'll translate it for you."

"Oh." Fernando shrugs. "I don't remember the title exactly. *Hidden Land. Secret Land.* Something like that. I found it interesting."

One thing I notice about grown-ups. A lot of times, they talk *around* things. They don't say straight out what's on their mind. So, you know what? I don't believe that was a real book plot he told us. I think it was *his* own theory. *He* believes that long, long ago, it all really happened.

And you know what *this* means, of course. Fernando believes *us!*

He looks at me. I look at him. *He* knows that *I* know that *he* knows. Still, we don't say it straight out. Aren't grown-ups strange? I guess he doesn't want to be taken for a crackpot if he said he believed our weird story — that glyptodons, and all the others, were still alive and well in Bolivia.

13.

Waiting

Now that Leo's on the mend, and everything's settling down, Mr. Valdez and my dad begin to think about the reason we're all here in the first place.

It seems the Bolivian government has a plan to build a big dam on the river to generate hydroelectric power.

My dad and Mr. Valdez want to inspect the dam site personally. They don't want to rely totally on official reports. They want to talk to local people before they try and decide whether the dam right in that spot is a good idea. Some people say no, because there's a lot of boat traffic on the river. That's important in the mountains, where the roads are so bad. After checking everything out, they — our dads — have to write an Environmental Impact Statement, listing the good points, and the bad points.

Early one morning, we waved them off. It was funny. Here were these two sophisticated energy experts, riding off on old bikes down a dirt road.

I've got to admit, though, I'm proud of my dad. It's important work. And he really can help people.

Part of the way, they were supposed to go on an ancient Inca trail over the mountains. I would have loved to go with them. But I didn't even ask. It would have been rotten for me to go off and leave Leo.

"Be careful, Bernardo," Mrs. Valdez sang out.

Mr. V turned around, nodded seriously, and blew her a kiss.

Leo and I sit around. He's still pretty weak. We play checkers. And shoot the breeze. We really got to know each other.

All this time, his mom keeps cooking huge meals. And stuffing us with all kinds of Bolivian goodies. My favorite was something they called salteña: a kind of pastry, with meat and olives and potatoes and raisins in it. The peanut soup was good, too. Fortunately, we were going to leave soon. Or else I would have looked like Fats Henderson by the time I got back home.

14.
Hasta la Vista

As soon as our dads came back, we flew off to La Paz. A letter from Fernando was waiting for me there. I ripped it open.

> Dear Alberto,
>   Sorry I could not say good-bye. I had to go back on Doc's plane, which was leaving in a hurry.
>   I have been thinking about what you asked me about dating . . .

(Dating! What is this! A "Dear Abby" letter? Then I knew. Of course! He wasn't talking about going out with girls. He was talking about argon potassium dating — to see how old a fossil is.) I read on:

I brought my dad's *Cordillerion* tusk fossil back with me. I am going to test it. The problem is, I don't want to go through normal channels. Which makes it a little harder. But I do have a good friend who works in the lab at the Instituto Científico. And Filipe can help me. But it will take time. I will write as soon as I know anything. Meanwhile, Hasta la vista.

Fernando McElderry

Holy moley! Great idea — to test the other tusk piece — the one his father found. Suppose they find out it's not two million years old? Suppose they find out it's brand new! Well, thirty years old. But that's like brand new when you're talking about prehistoric stuff.

Hasta la vista means "till I see you again." Hasta la vista to you, too, friend! What a guy!

Leo and I read the letter again.

"Caramba!" he said.

Caramba?

"You're going to have to learn more Spanish, pal. In your country, you would say, 'Wow!' Here, we say, Caramba!"

I folded up the letter. "It's gonna be hard keeping all this under our hats."

"Under our hats?"

I laughed. "And, you, my friend, are going to have to learn more American slang." I explained to Leo what it meant: keeping quiet about something.

We were on the patio. Leo sat down at the edge of the fountain. He stuck his hand under the water.

"Suppose Fernando tests the tusk . . . and it really turns out to be a few million years old? Just like they say."

I'd thought of that, too.

"But," I said, "that still doesn't mean we didn't see . . . you know."

Leo nodded. "I know. But who would pay attention to us if we didn't have something to corroborate our story?"

Whoa! Leo sure had some vocabulary! (I snuck a peak at the dictionary later on. Corroborate means "to back up with solid evidence.")

We had only three days left in La Paz. Time for Mr. Valdez and my dad to go to their energy conference. And for me to buy a present for my pal Fats.

I got him a charango. I bought it from a guy in the street. It's like a banjo. Only it's made from the shell of an armadillo. Fats is going to love it. (He plays the tuba in the school band.)

Suddenly, it was time to go. You know what? I hated to leave this place as much as I hated to come here.

The Valdezes saw us off at the airport. They hung around till our flight was called. Then we all hugged each other.

As we were about to board, I said to my mom, "Aren't you sorry you didn't let me go to baseball camp with Fats Henderson?"

Then I winked at Leo. We both knew we weren't really saying good-bye. We both

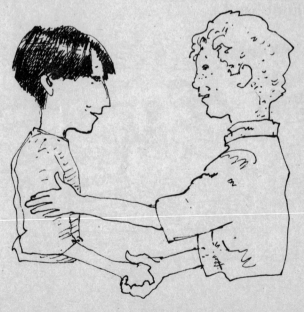

knew I'd come back. We knew we'd show them. Some day. When we have — what's that great thing that grown-ups always talk about? — credibility . . .

And then — with Fernando's help — we'll rediscover the secret land of the past. And this time, it would not be by accident.

Leo and I did our amigo handshake. Then I turned and boarded the plane.

Author's Note

Most of the strange animals that Alberto and Leo saw did exist in South America at one time. (Some, like saber-tooth, and the mastodon *Cordillerion*, lived until 10,000 years ago, or even more recently than that.)

How do we know these animals once lived in South America? Their fossil remains have been found there. All, that is, except for *Stegotetrabelodon*, the elephant with four tusks. So far, remains of four-tuskers have been found only in Africa.

Does that mean as an absolute fact that this particular kind of prehistoric elephant never lived in South America? No. All it means is that their fossils have never been found there. As you can guess, the fossil remains of every single animal that ever lived have not been found. So, as Alberto says, we cannot rule out the idea that four-tuskers once lived in South America. It's just that no one has ever found one there.

The Pleistocene Age, or Ice Age, was a time when many animals were gigantic in size. So, in the story, the boys were not exaggerating. Ground sloths, like "hu-mongous-orange," were twenty feet long. The armadillo-like *Glyptodon* ("armadillo-dragon") was fifteen feet long. (Ground sloths today are only about two feet long. Armadillos now measure around ten inches.)

Finally, is it possible for an animal believed to be extinct still to be alive today? Yes. A strange, six-foot-long prehistoric fish called the *Coelacanth* (SEAL a canth) was thought to have become extinct ninety million years ago. Then, amazingly, in 1938, a fisherman caught a live one in a net! This was off the east coast of South Africa. Since then, a few hundred more live ones have been found. So how can we absolutely be sure that somewhere, in some hidden place, saber-tooth, *Cordillerion,* and other prehistoric animals are still not alive?

It's not likely. But it's not impossible.